ICE AGE™
DAWN OF THE DINOSAURS

BUCK THE AMAZING DINO HUNTER!

HarperCollins®, 🎬®, and HarperEntertainment™ are trademarks of HarperCollins Publishers.

Ice Age: Dawn of the Dinosaurs: Buck the Amazing Dino Hunter!
Ice Age Dawn of the Dinosaurs ™ & © 2009 Twentieth Century Fox Film Corporation.

Library of Congress catalog card number: 2008942546
ISBN 978-0-06-168979-6
Typography by John Sazaklis
09 10 11 12 13 LP/CW 10 9 8 7 6 5 4 3 2 1
❖

First Edition

ICE AGE™
DAWN OF THE DINOSAURS

BUCK THE AMAZING DINO HUNTER!

ADAPTED BY
ANNIE AUERBACH

HARPER

ENTERTAINMENT

An Imprint of HarperCollinsPublishers

PROLOGUE

"There I was—my back against the wall, perched on the razor's edge of oblivion. . . ."

Buck the one-eyed weasel had his audience on the edge of their seats. The energetic animal with the eye patch knew how to tell a great story, especially one that was true.

"There was no way out," he continued. "I was staring into the heart of darkness."

The darkness was actually a gigantic white baryonyx's open mouth, framed by frighteningly sharp teeth, waiting to chomp down on the snack in front of him: a young Buck.

Just as the dinosaur named Rudy leaned in for the kill, Buck turned and leaped onto a long vine.

"Yahhh!" he cried, as he swung around a tree.

He let go, his hand in a fist as he flew right at Rudy. BAM! Rudy staggered backward from the blow, and Buck tumbled to the ground.

The dinosaur looked down, ready to stomp on Buck.

"Pop goes the weasel!" chimed Buck. He popped up, narrowly escaping Rudy's enormous foot.

The dinosaur's eyes blazed with fury. He swiped at Buck with his massive claws, swatting the weasel against a log. Buck looked up to see a tree falling toward him. Luckily, the tree missed the weasel, but it slammed into the other end of the log, launching Buck into the air. Soon he began to plummet . . . right toward Rudy's open jaws!

The group assembled around the campfire gasped. Ellie the mammoth was clutching Manny the mammoth's trunk, and the possums Crash and Eddie were hanging onto each other. Diego tried to pretend he wasn't interested, but the saber-toothed tiger really wanted to hear how the story ended.

Buck was happy to continue. "Never had I felt more alive than when I was so close to death," he said.

With his legs spread-eagle, Buck stared down into Rudy's throat. But before he was swallowed into the belly of the beast, Buck grabbed hold of Rudy's uvula—that pink thing that dangles in the back of the throat. He swung back and forth and back and forth. When he had enough momentum, he let go and shot right out of the dinosaur's mouth!

Buck's audience sighed with relief. Crash and Eddie were especially impressed.

"I may have lost my eye that day, but I got *this*." The possums gasped as Buck held up a giant white tooth.

"You are Super-Weasel!"

"Ultra-Weasel!"

Buck grinned proudly. Then he said, "Now let me tell you about the time I used a sharpened clamshell—"

Manny rolled his eyes and cut him off. "That's enough fairy tales for one night!"

CHAPTER ONE

Two days earlier . . .

Manny's trunk covered Ellie's eyes as he led her to a surprise. Sid the sloth and the possums followed behind them.

"Can I look now?" asked an excited Ellie.

"Easy," replied Manny. "Don't overexcite the baby."

"Manny, something's got to give!" complained Ellie. "I'm in my sixth trimester!" She was getting tired of being pregnant.

"Hey," said Manny, "we're majestic creatures. We have to, uh, marinate."

Finally, Manny uncovered Ellie's eyes. "Voilà!" he said. "A playground for Junior!"

Ellie looked around, stunned by what she saw: a perfect prehistoric playground! There were seesaws, vine swings, an obstacle course, and a circular slide made of ice.

Ellie gasped. "It's amazing!"

A twinkling caught her eye. An exquisite ice mobile dangled from a branch.

Ellie gazed lovingly at the frozen carvings of Manny, Ellie, and a baby mammoth.

"Oh, Manny," said Ellie, touched.

"I made it myself," admitted Manny. "It's our family."

Sid noticed his image wasn't on the mobile and frowned. "Hey, why aren't I up there?"

"You can be on ours," Eddie offered, holding up a mobile made of live spiders and lots of creepy dead creatures.

"You'd fit right in!" added Crash.

"Wasn't there a pond around here?" Ellie asked, looking around confusedly.

"I drained it," said Manny. "Only takes six inches of water for a baby to drown."

"You *do* know your baby's going to be a mammoth, right?" Sid said.

"Maybe on the outside," said Crash.

"But inside? All possum, baby!" Eddie declared.

Then Ellie noticed that the trees were padded with snowballs. "I don't believe it! You're trying to baby-proof nature," she said to Manny. "This is the world our baby's going to grow up in. You can't change that."

"Of course I can!" said Manny. "I'm the biggest thing on Earth!"

Ellie touched her belly suddenly. "Ooooh!"

"What? Is it happening? You're going into labor?" Manny babbled, frazzled and nervous.

"Manny," said Ellie. "It was just a kick!" She took his trunk and guided it to her belly. Manny relaxed.

Sid, however, rushed up to Ellie.

"Ooh, ooh, ooh! I want to feel!" said Sid. He flattened himself against Ellie's flank. "I don't feel anything—"

Whomp! The baby inside Ellie's belly kicked Sid right into a tree!

"I like you already, kid!" joked Crash. He gave Ellie's belly a high-five.

"Manny, you've got to relax," Ellie said earnestly. "The best way to protect our baby is to have all of our friends around us. . . . Wait, where's Diego?"

Everyone looked around. Where *was* Diego?

CHAPTER TWO

A gazelle nibbled on a patch of grass. He stopped suddenly, his ears perked up in alarm. The sleek creature looked around, determined it was safe, and returned to feeding. However, not far away, a saber-toothed tiger crouched low in the grass, stalking his prey. He stayed quiet, watching and waiting to pounce.

A moment later, the time had come.

With a skillful leap, Diego launched himself forward. In an instant, the gazelle took off. But the saber was in hot pursuit, his muscles pumping with every step. Diego was getting closer . . . and closer . . . He was just about to take the gazelle down and then . . .

Diego slowed down. Huffing and puffing, the big cat was wheezing and winded. He was forced to stop running altogether. The gazelle looked behind him and couldn't believe his eyes. This was never how a hunt ended!

"Whoo!" laughed the gazelle. "My hooves are burnin', baby!" He blew on his hooves, as if they were on fire from running so fast. "Look! I've got to tiptoe!"

Diego sighed, frustrated by the whole experience.

The gazelle danced around Diego. "Enjoy my rear view!" he said before scampering off.

Diego glared after him. He was miserable.

Meanwhile, back at the playground, Manny realized that the playground was kid-proofed, but not *Sid*-proofed. The sloth wanted to play with everything.

"Come on, Sid, I don't want you touching anything," Manny told him. "This place is for kids. Are you a kid? Wait, don't answer that."

Sid touched a sculpture anyway, and its head fell off. *Whoops.*

Just then, Diego appeared.

"There you are!" Manny said to him. "You missed the big surprise."

"Oh, right," Diego said, not really interested at all. "I'll check it out later.

Manny tried to play it off. "Okay, see ya."

Concerned, Ellie turned to Manny. "You know, I think there's something bothering Diego," she said.

"Nah, I'm sure everything's fine," said Manny.

"You should talk to him," urged Ellie.

"Guys don't talk to guys about guy problems," Manny

explained. "We just punch each other on the shoulder."

When Ellie just stared at him, Manny finally said, "Okay, okay. I'm going."

Manny found Diego looking out at the expansive tundra. An awkward silence filled the air, broken only by Manny punching Diego's shoulder.

"Ow! Why'd you do that?" asked Diego.

"I don't know," Manny replied.

After another few moments of uncomfortable silence, Manny spoke. "So, listen, Ellie thinks there's something bothering you. But I told her—"

Diego interrupted him. "Actually, I've been thinking that maybe soon it might be time for me to head out . . . you know, on my own."

Manny wasn't sure what to make of that.

"Look, who are we kidding, Manny?" said Diego. "I'm not a kitty cat. I'm a saber. You think I'm going to chaperone playdates?"

"What are you talking about?" asked Manny.

"Having a family, that's huge. And I'm happy for you," continued Diego, "but that's your adventure, not mine."

Manny was offended. "You don't want to be around my kid?"

"You're taking this the wrong way," said Diego, shaking his head.

"Well, go find some adventure, Mr. Adventure Guy,"

Manny said, obviously hurt. "Don't let my boring domestic life hit you in the butt on the way out."

Manny stomped away from Diego. Sid, who had been listening, popped out. "Manny, wait!" he called desperately. "No one has to go anywhere."

But Manny kept walking. As he met Ellie he said, "See? That's why guys don't talk to guys."

"Why? What happened?" asked Ellie.

"Diego's leaving," replied Manny, as he walked away.

Sid looked at Diego. "Whoa, whoa, whoa!" he exclaimed. "This should be the best time of our lives. We're having a baby."

Diego shook his head. "No, Sid. *They're* having a baby."

"But we're a herd, a family," Sid said.

"Look, things have changed. Manny has other priorities now," Diego said. "Face it, Sid. We had a great run. But now it's time to move on."

Sid took a deep breath. "So it's just the two of us?"

"No, Sid. It's not the two of us."

"Crash and Eddie are coming with us?" Sid asked hopefully.

Diego shook his head. He turned and left.

Sid was stunned. He watched Diego walk away. He watched Manny walk away with Ellie. His family was crumbling. Where did he belong?

CHAPTER THREE

Sid trudged along the frozen tundra. Up to his knees in snow, the sloth was all alone and trying to keep it together.

"Okay, calm down," he repeated to himself. "I'm good at making friends. I'll make my own herd."

But when he tried, the birds flew away, gophers dived into their holes, even the glyptodons shrunk back into their shells.

Sid sighed in despair. He looked down at his reflection in the glassy ice. "Well, at least you've still got your looks."

CRACK! The ice Sid was standing on gave way, and he dropped onto an ice shelf below. The strange underground chamber looked stark and empty until Sid came upon three enormous, perfectly shaped eggs.

"Hello?" Sid said timidly. His voice echoed throughout the chamber. He moved closer to the eggs, looking at them tenderly. "Aw, poor guys. I know what it's like to feel abandoned." He brushed dirt off one of them. "Don't worry, you're not alone anymore."

Before long, Sid heaved the eggs out of the ice shelf and began rolling them one by one. When one out-of-control egg rolled toward a set of jagged rocks, Sid couldn't stop it. Luckily, Ellie came to the rescue, snatching the runaway egg with her trunk just in time.

"Oh, thank you, thank you!" Sid gushed to Ellie. Then he turned to the egg. "Bad egg! Rotten egg! You almost gave me a heart attack!" He stopped and hugged the egg. "I'm sorry, darling. I'm just a little scrambled. It's just that I love you so much. Now I want you to meet your uncle Manny and aunt Ellie."

Sid presented the eggs to the mammoths. Each egg

had a smiley face drawn on it. "I'd like to present Egbert, Shelly, and Yoko."

"Whatever you're doing, it's a bad idea," Manny said to Sid.

Sid covered one of the egg's "ears" and said, "Shh! My kids'll hear you!"

"They're not your kids, Sid," said Manny. "Take them back. You're not meant to be a parent."

"Why not?" Sid asked innocently.

Manny looked squarely at the sloth, "First sign? Stealing someone else's eggs. Second sign? One of them almost became an omelet."

"Someone's probably worried sick looking for them," Ellie piped up.

Sid explained to the mammoths that the eggs were abandoned. "If it weren't for me, they'd be *kidsicles*."

Manny softened. "Sid, I know what you're going through. And you'll have a family, too, someday."

"Oh, I get it," Sid interrupted. He was bitterly disappointed. "You have your family, and I'm better off alone. By myself. A fortress of solitude. In the ice. Forever. A lone, lonely loner."

As Sid walked away, feeling dejected and miserable, Ellie looked at Manny. She was concerned.

While Sid pushed the eggs across the snow on a sled, he said to them, "Why should I take you back? I love kids. I'm responsible, loving, nurturing. What do you think?" When there was no response from the eggs, Sid smiled and said, "I knew you would agree."

CHAPTER FOUR

The next morning Sid woke up under the shelter of a rocky ledge. He yawned, stretched, and finally opened his eyes. To Sid's astonishment, gazing down at him were three adorable baby *dinosaurs*!

"Momma!" cried the dinos, each nearly half the size of Sid.

Sid's eyes lit up. "I'm a mommy!" he cried happily. Sid took good care of the youngsters, bathing and feeding them. He played peekaboo with them and loved every minute. They walked by the playground Manny had built, and the dinos looked at the slide longingly. They wanted to play, but the gate was closed.

"That's just for kids," Sid explained. "Wait a minute!" he exclaimed. "You *are* kids!" He opened the gate, adding, "Just don't break anything."

The baby dinos happily bounded in.

Just then, a young animal who had been watching shouted, "The sloth says the playground's open!"

"No, wait! Not for everyone!" Sid shouted back. But it was too late. Young animals of all ages and species ran in from the woods, stampeding Sid. Panicked, he ran around, trying to control the situation. "No, no, no! Don't touch that!"

Some of the moms huddled together, pointing at the dinos. A beaver boy hung onto a baby dinosaur's tail as it ran by.

"What are they?" asked the mole-hog mom.

One of the baby dinosaurs was fighting the little beaver girl for a stick. "Mommy!" called a beaver girl. "He's not sharing."

The girl's mother looked at Sid. "Aren't you going to do something?"

Sid looked frazzled. "I'm a single mother with three kids. I could use a little compassion!"

But there was no time for compassion. Just then, a mole-hog kid screamed, "Slow down! Please!"

Sid saw that one of the baby dinosaurs was whipping the mole-hog kids around too fast inside a turtle shell. The shell started shooting the kids into the air. As Sid tried to catch one of the kids, he also saw one of the dinos pushing a terrified boy way too high on the vine swings.

"Stop! Stop! Stop!" pleaded the kid. The dino didn't understand and pushed the boy so hard that the kid flew out of the park.

"Ronald!" screamed his mother.

"Oh, that's a shame," Sid said, shaking his head. He looked around nervously. Things were out of control.

Sid watched as the other two dinos rushed up to the slide. One pushed little Johnny, an aardvark boy, down the slide, while the second dino stood at the bottom—with his mouth wide open!

"Ahh!" cried Johnny.

Johnny's mom screamed as Johnny slid down the slide and became the baby dinosaur's breakfast!

All the mothers screamed and shepherded their kids from the playground. Sid marched over to the dino that ate Johnny.

"Come on, spit him out," Sid said sternly.

The dino shook his head defiantly.

Sid put his hands on his hips. "If you don't spit out little Johnny, we're leaving the playground this instant. One . . . two . . . don't make me say three."

The dino spit out a few other creatures before finally spitting out little Johnny. The aardvark mom scooped up her slime-covered boy and fled, just as Manny and Ellie entered.

Manny looked around in horror. What had happened to his pristine playground? Even the ice mobile had shattered to the ground.

"I'm really sorry," Sid said, sheepishly. "The important

thing is that no one got hurt." He looked around and frowned. "Except for that guy. And those three. And her."

Manny's shock turned to anger. "I told you to take them back, and you kept them! Now look what they've done!"

"Okay, granted, we do have some discipline issues—" began Sid.

"Eating kids is not a discipline issue!" roared Manny.

"But he spit them out!" argued Sid.

"Well, that's super. Let's give him a gold star. Kid of the week!" replied Manny. He put his face right up to Sid's. "They don't belong here. Whatever they are, wherever you found them, take them back."

Sid stood up to Manny. "I'm not getting rid of my kids."

Before they could argue anymore, the earth began to rumble. Was it an earthquake? The animals looked around anxiously. They felt a sudden violent jolt and then heard an ear-piercing shriek.

"Do earthquakes shriek?" yelled Crash, as he ran for cover.

The shriek was followed by a huge roar, which echoed through the valley. It belonged to a mother Tyrannosaurus rex looking for her children! Everyone shook with fear.

"I thought dinosaurs were extinct," said Ellie.

"Then that is one angry fossil!" replied Manny, as he led Ellie to safety.

In a nearby cave, the baby dinos were scared by the noise. Sid tried to comfort them and keep them from crying, but it wasn't working. The mother dinosaur headed toward the sound.

RIIIIIP! The mother dinosaur tore the top off the cave in which Sid and the babies were huddled together.

"Sid! Give them to her!" Manny called from behind a nearby rock. "She's their mother."

"How do I know she's their mother?" Sid called back.

"You want a birth certificate?" yelled Manny.

Sid stood firm. He looked straight at the mother

dinosaur and declared, "These are *my* kids, and you're going to have to go through me to get them."

The mother dinosaur cocked her head in thought. All the animals watching held their breath. Then the dinosaur reached down and used her mouth to scoop up her kids— and Sid, too!

CHAPTER FIVE

Out on the plains, a gazelle ran by Diego. "Run!" the animal called.

Diego gave an annoyed sigh. "Don't you have anything better to do?" he said.

ROAAR! The mother dinosaur charged across the plains with Sid and the three young dinos in her mouth.

"Help!" cried Sid.

Diego was thoroughly confused. "Sid?"

While Diego was trying to figure out what he had just seen, the rest of the gang peered into the massive hole in the ground from which the mother dinosaur had emerged and then disappeared into again.

"Sid must be down there," said Manny.

Jagged rocks sloped down into darkness. Mysterious wisps of steam rose up. Crash and Eddie were eager to make their exit. But Ellie wasn't going home without Sid.

Manny insisted Ellie and the possums return home. He told her that she shouldn't be running around strange caves in her condition.

But Ellie was determined. She brushed by him and started the descent into the hole. The others had no choice but to follow. Inside the eerie cavern, the group ran into a familiar face.

"Diego?" said Manny. "What are you doing down here?"

"Vacationing," Diego replied sarcastically. Then he added, "Same as you. Looking for Sid."

Manny opened his mouth to say something, but Ellie cut him off. "Great! We need all the help we can get," she said warmly.

The group headed to the right, where a warm shaft

of light shone through. As they moved into the light, their breath caught in their throats. There in front of them stood a vast jungle—full of massive dinosaurs, prehistoric vegetation, rivers of lava, and even tar pits. A thick layer of ice hung above as their sky.

"We've been living above an entire world, and we didn't even know it," said Ellie. She was awestruck.

"I feel so puny," said Manny.

Crash looked up at the big mammoth. "How do you think *I* feel?"

Suddenly, the huge spiked tail of an angry anklyosaurus slammed down in front of them.

"Run for it!" yelled Ellie. "Hurry!"

The group ran over a bridge, but found a dead end. The anklyosaurus was looming over them, opening its mouth, when Ellie spotted something. She saw a humongous dinosaur called a diplodocus munching on some tree leaves nearby. Thinking quickly, Ellie ripped a juicy frond from a plant and held it out to the diplodocus.

"Here, boy!" she called and whistled.

The long-necked diplodocus approached Ellie and happily took the frond in its mouth.

"Climb on," Ellie urged to the group.

"We're not getting on that thing!" insisted Manny.

"It's this dinosaur or that one," said Ellie, pointing to the charging anklyosaurus.

Without a moment to lose, the group jumped onto the diplodocus's head as it rose over the vista. They each slid down the dinosaur's neck and body, all the way to the tail, landing in a pile on the ground.

They looked around. They were surrounded by huge dinosaurs staring down at them. It looked like they were about to be lunch, when they met Buck.

"*Aaaa-ya-ah-yaaaa-ya-ah-yaaa!*" yelled the weasel, as he swung in on a vine right between the dinosaurs and the gang. He was wearing twig camouflage and an ammunition belt made of different fruits. Buck threw a series of fruit bombs to create a smoke screen. "Fire in the hole!"

A white cloud covered the group and they made their

escape. They were safe, for now.

CHAPTER SIX

As Buck the one-eyed weasel led the weary travelers through the jungle, he asked what they were doing there.

"Our friend was taken by a dinosaur," explained Ellie.

"A giant one," added Crash. "All *arrgggh* and *grrrr*!" He stomped his feet and reared his head back for effect.

Buck nodded. "I know her. She came through carrying some floppy green thing."

"We're friends with the floppy green thing," said Manny.

"Well, he's dead," Buck said bluntly. "Now go home."

"Not without Sid," Ellie said with determination.

Just then, Diego spotted tracks. Everyone ran to look

at the huge dinosaur tracks that led into the bush.

"She's going to Lava Falls. That's where they care for their newborns," said Buck. "To get there, you've got to go through the Jungle of Misery, across the Chasm of Death, to the Plains of Woe."

Buck turned to a nearby plant as if it *had* said something. "What? The mammoth?" he said to the plant. "Yeah, he's a fat one. They'll eat him first."

"I'm not fat—it's my fur!" insisted Manny. "It's poofy."

Diego nudged him. "Manny, he's talking to a bush."

"We'll leave you two to talk," Manny said to Buck and his friend the bush.

Buck realized no one was taking him seriously. "You think this is some tropical getaway?" he said to Manny. "You may have been the biggest animal back home, but down here you're just an appetizer."

Diego chuckled at that.

"Don't laugh, tiger," Buck told Diego. "You're dessert." To Crash and Eddie he said, "You two are after-dinner mints."

Crash thought about that for a second and said, "Refreshing!"

Manny had heard enough. He pushed Buck aside. "All right, we get it. Doom and despair. Yadda yadda."

As Buck watched the group go into the bush, he simply shook his head. "Meals on heels. That's all they are in there. Meals on heels."

The group trekked through thick foliage, finally emerging into a lush field of beautiful, tropical plants. No one noticed that, as they walked, the giant plants turned toward them, tracking their every step.

Ellie huffed and puffed. "Hold on," she announced.

"Why? What's wrong?" Manny asked nervously. He used his trunk to feel Ellie's forehead.

"I've got a funny feeling. Something's not right," she said, sensing something odd about the area.

"You're hungry!" guessed Manny. "Low blood sugar! There's some fruit." He dashed toward a bush.

"I wouldn't do that if I were you," warned Diego. "This isn't exactly your playground."

Manny snorted. "Like I'm really going to be afraid of a pretty flower."

The mammoth reached out to grab some fruit when a vine coiled around his foot.

"Uh, the pretty flower's squeezing me," said Manny.

"Very funny," Diego said, rolling his eyes.

"Do I sound like I'm joking?" Manny cried, panic creeping into his voice.

"All right, stay still. I'll get the big bad flower off you," said Diego, stifling a laugh.

As he tried to help Manny, a vine coiled around Diego's leg. Then both animals were yanked up into the air.

"Not so funny now, is it, Chuckles?" Manny said.

"Manny!" screamed Ellie, as the vines hurled them over to the middle of an enormous blossom. The huge petals began to rise and fully engulfed the pair. The plant was about to devour them!

"That's it," said Ellie. "I'm tearing it up from the roots."

"Do that, and it'll clamp shut forever," said a voice.

It was Buck. He sprang into action. "Don't worry. I'll have them out of there before they're digested."

Manny poked his head out of the plant. *"Digested?"* He and Diego began to scream as the plant's digestive juices started to rise.

There was very little time left. Buck lathered himself up

with goo to protect himself from the plant's liquids. Then he took a leap and dived right into the dastardly petals.

Inside, Buck worked his way down to the bottom of the plant and cut the yellow stalks that grew in the center. The plant shuddered, and then one by one, the petals unfurled and the digestive juices splashed out—along with Manny and Diego, who gasped for air. Although they were covered in goo, they were happy to be alive. Buck stood triumphantly on top of them.

With Ellie's urging, Manny and Diego shuffled up to Buck.

"Uh, thank you for saving us," Manny mumbled. Then he nudged Diego.

"What he said," said Diego.

Ellie rolled her eyes. She walked up to Buck. "What they're trying to say is, we need you. Will you help us find Sid?"

Buck turned and looked seriously at the group. "From now on, my habitat, my rules. Rule number one: *Always* listen to Buck. Rule number two: Stay in the middle of the trail. Rule number three: He who has gas travels in the back of the pack."

Eddie guiltily retreated to the back.

"Now let's move out!" said Buck, as he headed into the bush.

"We should have our heads examined," Manny said, as he and the others followed.

Buck yelled to him. "That's rule number four!"

Diego caught up to Buck. "So, you're just living down here by your wits? All alone, no responsibilities?"

"Yep," Buck replied proudly. "It's incredible. No dependents, no limits. It's the greatest life a single guy could have."

Diego thought that sounded pretty good—until Buck picked up a rock and started talking to it as if it were alive.

Manny walked by and whispered to Diego, "That's you in three weeks."

Diego growled as he followed the others.

That night, Buck told them the story of his historic fight with Rudy the dinosaur and how one small weasel came to possess one large, dinosaur snaggletooth.

The gang went to sleep with visions of drooling, vicious dinosaurs in their heads. They had no idea how soon their dreams would come true.

CHAPTER SEVEN

In another part of the jungle, Sid and the mother dinosaur were figuring out their family issues. Despite Sid's insistence that he care for the youngsters, the mother dinosaur wanted her babies to herself. And Sid wanted to be anything but lunch.

"Listen, families get complicated," Sid said. "Maybe we can work something out, Momma."

CHOMP! Momma lunged at Sid, who dodged behind some vines.

"If you eat me, it will send a bad message to the kids!" Sid pleaded.

Momma didn't care. She stomped toward the helpless

Sid. At the last moment, a surprising thing happened. The three baby dinos shielded Sid.

This confused their mother. She took a step back.

Sid raised his arm in a triumphant pose. "Score one for the sloth!"

The next day, the group continued their journey to find their friend. Ellie had already reached a safe alcove in the rocks, and the rest were climbing up after her when an earth-shattering roar echoed in the distance.

"Rudy!" said Buck. The vicious dinosaur was on the hunt.

Then came a high-pitched scream. *"AAAAAAHHHH!"*

"Never heard that kind of dino before," Buck said, scratching his head.

"That's Sid!" exclaimed Manny.

"They must be over by Lava Falls," said Buck. "We'll have to move fast."

"Manny!" Ellie screamed, panic in her voice.

"We're coming!" Manny called to her.

Ellie inhaled sharply, feeling something moving. She yelled out to Manny. "You'd better hurry . . . 'cause the baby's coming, too!"

The others froze in shock.

Buck took control. "There's only one thing to do." He turned to Crash and Eddie. "Possums, you're with me. Manny, take care of Ellie until we get back."

Manny freaked out. "You can't leave now!" he said to Buck. "She's off the trail! What about rule number two?"

"Rule number five says you can ignore rule number two if there's a female involved, or possibly a cute dog," began Buck. "You know, I just make up these rules as I go along."

"Yeah—but she's—you have to—" Manny babbled nervously.

Diego stepped up. "It's all right. I got your back."

With that, Buck took the possums and leaped off a cliff. A few seconds later, a pterodactyl rose up above the cliff with Buck and the possums on its back. It was time to rescue the sloth.

CHAPTER EIGHT

Buck, Crash, and Eddie soared through the sky on the pterodactyl's back. Buck swiftly maneuvered between the other pterodactyls, who were on the hunt for possums.

Finally, they spotted Sid on a rock in a river of hot lava. The sloth desperately hopped from rock to rock, trying to get away from the huge lava falls. But he ran out of rocks! Just as the current began to pull him over the edge of the falls, the pterodactyl snatched Sid up in its talons. The sloth cried out for help until he looked up and saw Crash and Eddie.

"I can't believe it!" Sid exclaimed. "I never thought I'd see you again!"

Eddie explained that the whole gang was there looking for him. Sid was touched.

The pterodactyl flew right past the mother and baby dinosaurs. Seeing Sid, Momma shrieked and charged after them.

"Wait! My kids! I have to say good-bye!" exclaimed Sid.

"No time, soldier," replied Buck, as they narrowly made their escape.

Meanwhile, the rest of the gang was facing other dangers. A pack of vicious dinosaurs, called guanlongs, was heading toward Ellie. Manny wanted to run to Ellie, but Diego stopped him.

"You hold those guys back. I can get to Ellie faster," said Diego. He looked Manny in the eye. "You have to trust me."

Manny looked at the approaching guanlongs and then up at Ellie. He turned to Diego and took the biggest leap of faith. "All right. Let's do it."

The friends sprang into action. Diego leaped up the boulders, getting to Ellie in record time. He fought back any gualongs that made it past Manny.

On the rocks below, Manny heroically fought the guanlongs with his tusks and his sheer weight. It was a fierce battle, but as soon as Manny heard the first cry of his newborn baby, adrenaline filled the mammoth and he made his ascent into the alcove.

Manny ran to Ellie, relieved to see she was all right. When Manny saw the adorable newborn, his heart melted. He reached down and stroked the baby with his trunk. Everyone was moved. Even Diego shed a tear.

"I saw that, tough guy," Ellie teased.

Diego tried to cover. "That last dino caught my eye with a claw and—"

The others looked skeptical.

"All right, I'm not made of stone!" Diego admitted, with a small smile.

Manny looked squarely at Diego. The mammoth's smile showed his gratitude to Diego for being such a huge help.

"Incoming!" came a voice.

The friends turned to see a pterodactyl flying right at them. They were thrilled to see Sid swinging in its talons. Sid, Buck, and the possums were excited to meet the new baby mammoth.

Sid already had baby name ideas. "Sidney is a wonderful name for a girl," he suggested.

"I think one Sid is about all the world can handle," Ellie said lightly. She looked down at the baby. "Right, Peaches?"

"Peaches. I love it," said Manny.

Watching nearby, Buck sighed. "I'm really going to miss you guys. I forgot what it was like to be part of a family," he said. Then he straightened his eye patch. "All right, mammals, let's get you home."

CHAPTER NINE

Led by Buck, the reunited friends were about to make their way toward the original cavern to get back home.

THWACK! A massive tail swept Buck into the air. The others looked up to see an enormous, white dinosaur. His massive battle-scarred head blocked out the sun. As he bared his teeth, they saw his missing tooth.

"Rudy!" exclaimed Manny. He now realized that Buck was telling the truth about battling the dangerous dinosaur.

Buck spotted some giant moths in the rocks. "Shoo! Shoo!" he called to them.

The moths took to the air, swarming around Rudy. The

dinosaur staggered backward, trying to swat them away.

Buck seized the moment to slip out of Rudy's claw and drop to the ground. He squinted up at the dinosaur. "Let's rhumba."

Rudy squinted back, his tongue slithering around the gap in his teeth. Then he gave an earth-shattering roar and lunged after the weasel, but Buck cartwheeled out of the way in time. Then Buck grabbed a stinkbug, pulled the pin, and . . . nothing happened. It was a dud!

"That's a problem," said Buck.

Rudy flung Buck out of the way. Then he turned on the rest of the group, licking his chops.

Suddenly, an angry shriek echoed throughout the jungle. It didn't come from Rudy—it came from Momma! Rudy turned, but it was too late. Momma knocked him back with a headbutt to his chest.

"Way to go, *Mom-zilla!*" Sid cheered. He was delighted that she had come to protect Sid. And her babies were pretty proud, too.

Rudy got to his feet and faced off against Momma.

The two gigantic monsters clawed and snapped at each other. They whipped at each other with their tails.

As the battle raged on, Manny and Diego led Ellie, Peaches, and the possums down the rocks, out of harm's way. Sid and the baby dinos took cover behind a large rock.

Rudy gave Momma a hard swipe, and she went down. He loomed over her. Was this the end of Momma?

Suddenly, Rudy went down! The baby dinos had attacked his feet, causing the vicious dinosaur to fall over. Buck, eager to get into the fray, grabbed a vine and lassoed Rudy's snout while he was on the ground. Rudy struggled to get to his feet, thrashing his head and whipping Buck off his snout.

When Momma saw Rudy kicking the dinos off, she filled with rage. No one messed with her babies! She charged, knocking Rudy through a rock pillar and right over the edge of a deep crevasse. A final roar could be heard as Rudy vanished into the void.

"Oh, thank you, Momma!" Sid cried, rushing up to

her. "Thank you!" He watched as the baby dinos nuzzled next to their mother. Sid was moved.

"You're where you belong now," Sid said to the baby dinos. "And I'm sure you'll grow up to be giant, horrifying dinosaurs . . . just like your mother." Then he looked at Momma and added, "Take good care of our kids."

Momma leaned over and licked Sid's hair into a Mohawk. She threw her head back and unleashed a sad good-bye roar. Sid did the same, but it sounded more like gargling. He sighed sadly as he watched the dinosaurs go.

"They grow up so fast," Sid said, shaking his head. "I mean, it seems like they were born one day and gone the next."

"They were, Sid," Diego pointed out.

"Yeah, that was a lot of work," said Sid.

Manny knew it wasn't easy for Sid to give up the kids. "You were a good parent, Sid," Manny told him. And he meant it.

"Thanks," replied Sid. "Can I babysit for you?"

Without missing a beat, Manny answered, "Not a chance."

"I work cheap," offered Sid.

"All right. I'll think about it," replied Manny. Then he whispered to Diego, "Never happen."

Meanwhile, Buck stared down at the crevasse where Rudy had fallen. "He's gone," said Buck, looking bewildered. "What am I supposed to do now?"

"Come with us," suggested Ellie.

Everyone agreed, and Buck felt flattered. "Wow. I never thought of going back. I've been down here so long. I'm not sure if I can fit in up there anymore."

"So," said Diego. "Look at us. We look like a normal herd to you?"

Buck took a thoughtful look at them: three mammoths, two possums, one saber-toothed tiger, and one sloth.

"All right, I'm in!" Buck decided.

One by one, they headed through the cavern toward the Ice Age. At the back of the line was Buck. He took one last long look back, straining to hear something. But it didn't come.

"So long, Rudy," said Buck with a sigh. He started walking up the final step when he heard a faint roar. An ecstatic smile crossed Buck's face. Rudy was alive!

Buck looked up at Diego, who was waiting for him. "I've got to—"

Diego nodded. He understood that the adventure needed to continue for Buck.

Buck took out his knife. "This world should really stay down here," he said, and cut through the key joint of the bridge to the Ice Age. As the bridge buckled and swayed, Buck had one final rule for Diego: "Take care of 'em, tiger."

Diego saluted and grinned. "Always listen to Buck!"

Buck held onto a vine as the bridge collapsed, sending the weasel swinging back into the dinosaur world.

Manny, Diego, and the others scrambled out of the cavern just before it collapsed. They were back in the Ice Age. They were home.

CHAPTER TEN

"We made it!" cheered Eddie. He bent over and kissed the ice, his lips getting stuck. Once Crash helped him get unstuck, he looked around. "Where's Buck?" he asked.

"Don't worry. He's where he wants to be," said Diego, realizing he felt the exact same way.

"Do you think he's okay?" Crash asked, worried for the weasel.

Diego laughed. "Are you kidding? Nothing could kill that weasel. It's Rudy I'm worried about!"

Ellie put Peaches down on the ice. The sweet baby mammoth stared to slide, but Ellie was there to help her. Manny and Diego watched nearby.

"I know this 'baby makes three' thing isn't for you,"

Manny began to say to Diego.

The saber interrupted him. "I'm not leaving, buddy," said Diego. "Life of adventure? It's right here."

Manny was taken aback. "But I've got a whole speech here. I've been working on it!" he said. "How can I show you that I'm strong and sensitive, noble yet caring?"

Diego thought a moment and then gave Manny a punch on the shoulder.

"Ow!" said Manny. He grinned at Diego. "Thanks."

Ellie smiled, grateful that the gang was back together again, along with a new addition. Peaches didn't know it yet, but she was one lucky little mammoth—she had been born into a big family!